Yesterday Island

Renee Hart

Impassioned Romance Books

D1470510

ISBN-13: 978-1541045842

ISBN-10: 154104584X

Other Alaska Adventure Books by Renee Hart

A Single Year

The Summer Nanny

End Of The Road

Together In The Wild

Something Wild in Anchorage

Table of Contents

Yesterday Island

An Alaska Adventure Novella

Description: After all of Kat's friends and siblings were married, they made it their job to find her a husband. Then her company had to lay her off along with a third of the workforce.

Kat needed to find work far away from her meddling friends and family. She found a teaching position at a grade school on Yesterday Island, a small island in the Bering Strait.

In a story that weaves the past with the present, Kat is taken under the wing of the local peace officer. He introduces her to a new friend who opens the door to learning about two young people from the past and how their story affected the present day lives of the people on Yesterday Island.

Yesterday Island

Chapter One

Kat looked around the drab room and sighed. Like it or not, this was going to be her home for the next nine months. The nondescript color of the walls matched the floor and most of the furnishings. The one bright spot in the room was her pile of suitcases stacked in the corner. She rested her eyes upon them for a moment as she thought about the reasons for such a drastic move.

There was no denying that five weddings in the last three years had pushed her to make some kind of change. Two of the brides were her younger twin sisters and they'd opted for a double wedding to save their father some money.

The other three brides were the mainstay of her circle of friends from high school. One by one, they'd said their vows and slipped into another kind of life that didn't lend itself to crashing on each other's couches and middle of the night calls for no reason beyond the need to talk to someone.

Kat was the last among her friends to find someone willing to make that kind of commitment. It turned out that most of the men she'd dated were less interested in commitments than her. She could remember the long, late night conversations where her friends had vowed to remain single forever, or at least as long as possible. Eventually they were all forced them to eat those vows, leaving her as the sole survivor on the behalf of freedom from marriage.

Her friends and family saw her "freedom" as a cause to be taken up and they all turned into yentas. Every dinner invitation was suspect as she found herself face to face with strange men chosen by distant relatives and their various workplaces. She pushed back against these efforts by showing up in sweats or making lame excuses, but her friends were relentless.

The final blow to her freedom came when the company she considered herself committed to for the long haul was forced to lay off more than a third of the workforce after a hostile takeover.

Kat was only a junior member on the editing staff and was near the top of the list of those axed. It didn't matter that she'd given nearly ten years of her life to building her reputation there. The new owners weren't interested in reputations. They were looking for a quick return on their investment. Out with the old and in with the new was their motto.

With little savings and a weak job market, Kat was faced with the prospect of having to move back home with her parents. The thought of giving up her apartment for her old room was too depressing to think about and Kat decided to search the internet to find some kind of alternative lifestyle to fill in this employment gap.

Her childhood dream was to be a teacher. That was replaced by a college dream of becoming a writer. Since college, her only writing was limited to the editing work she'd done on the job. With that job out of the picture, Kat figured it might be worth exploring the earlier dream of being a teacher. However, she didn't want the usual kind of job at a nearby school. With her friends determined to find her a husband, she wanted to get as far away from them and her family as possible.

She pored over job listings for faraway countries on the internet where opportunities were presented in glowing terms. The idea of moving to the other side of the globe looked great on a computer screen. Being a practical young woman, she wasn't ready to take that big of a leap of faith, however, and she narrowed her search to Alaska.

She found plenty of interesting postings for teachers in the native villages. The place that really captured her imagination was a small island that lay in the Bering Strait called Yesterday Isle. The past was where her heart longed to stay.

She applied for the job and much to her surprise, her application was accepted without so much as an interview. She found herself with an expected date of arrival in Alaska post haste.

Flying to Anchorage wasn't all that different from flying to any other large city in the U.S. Kat arrived in the middle of the night, so her first impression wasn't very impressive at all. The next day, she was scheduled to meet up with the rest of the teachers to complete their journey to the island. Her whirlwind decision to change her life was in full hurricane mode at this point and she'd barely caught her breath after saying good-bye to the old one.

After a few hours of sleep at a cheap motel, Kat felt as chipper as a block of wood. Her breakfast meeting of her fellow colleagues gave her little time to determine anything about them. It was only clear that she was the newbie and had no idea of what she had taken on with this job. It had also come out that the reason she'd been given the job was because no one else had applied and they needed to fill the position immediately. This news did little to inspire her to feel confident about her own skills.

There was little time to take in more than a few passing views of mountains and trees before their group was loaded into a small plane to fly to Nome. From there, the small group would be transported to the island on a ferry, and that was heavily dependent on the weather conditions. Kat struggled to keep track of her bags and cases as things were poked and pushed into the most unlikely places.

Space was clearly limited on the small plane. The other three passengers were accustomed to the cramped conditions and made every effort to stow things in a way to make themselves a bit more comfortable. Kat realized that inexperience had left her sharing seating space with a large case of spaghetti and her heavy tote bag. Looking around at the others, she wondered if her discomfort was deliberate, but found no one hogging an excess of room.

"Here, let me move that this way a little more," the young man sitting behind her said over her shoulder. "Then, you can put your tote on top of the case. At least you'll be able to walk when we arrive in Nome," he laughed.

"Thanks," she tossed back as the two of them

wrestled the case more towards the center.

"My name's Jim, by the way," he added as if she'd somehow forgotten their earlier meeting.

"Kat."

"Ah, yes. And that was Kat with a "K", if I remember correctly," Jim said.

"Correct."

"And what is it that has Kat with a "K" running away to Yesterday Isle," he asked by way of conversation, "if you don't mind me asking, that is?"

"What makes you think I'm running away," Kat asked.

"I'm not sure yet," he added. "It's just a feeling."

"Leave her alone, Jim," the young woman sitting across from them said bluntly. "She's not your type."

"Oh? And what type would that be, Marissa," Jim sneered.

The glance that passed between the two of them made it clear to Kat there was a history here and it hadn't ended all that well from the looks of things. The chill in the air put an end to the conversation, which was fine with Kat as the pilot revved up the engines for take-off. The noise level inside the plane left little chance for intelligible conversation anyway. Kat double-checked her seat belt and then laughed to herself. The belt wasn't going to make much of a difference if they crashed. The packages and baggage crammed inside the plane would kill them all no matter how they stayed in their seats. She choked down the regrets rising up inside of her and turned to look out the window. *There was no room in this whirlwind for turning back*, she thought to herself as her stomach twisted. *I'm just going to have to make the best of this.*

***

Iliana wiped her muddy hands on the front of her tunic and laughed when Ulriq did the same. She knew her mother would be angry at the state of her clothes, but Papa never cared. He always said children should get dirty when they played or they weren't having any fun. Her mother would just grumble until Papa would sweep her into his arms and kiss her complaints away. The two of them never stayed angry for very long. Their love was too important to be squandered on petty squabbles.

The two children ran to the top of the bluff and crouched down behind the rocks to spy on the men below. The boat men were busy loading large bundles of furs and hides onto the longboats and both Iliana and Ulriq knew exactly what that meant to them. Their short time together was about to end and Iliana would leave with her parents back across the narrow strait into the land that lay beyond the dark water.

They were silent as they watched the activity below. Nothing either of them could say would make any difference to the situation. It was the same every year. In the silence, their hands sought each other and they gripped the other tightly as if somehow they could hold on to this moment forever.

"Iliana," Ulriq said as he turned to lean his back against the rock, "promise me you will come back again next year."

"You know that even if I promised you, there's nothing I can do to make my father return. He only comes for the hides and furs. He doesn't care about anything else."

"That's not true," Ulriq retorted. "I know he loves you and if you begged him, he might come for that reason."

Iliana laughed as she jumped up and ran away from the bluff.

"You'd do better to ask him to promise," she called back over her shoulder. "He loves you too!"

Ulriq chased after her and the two of them ran and ran until their breath would no longer come and they flopped to the ground and lay there panting. They both knew the island wasn't big enough for them to run far enough to stop the inevitable. It was the same every year when Iliana's father would bring his family to the island to trade with the People for the hides and furs they gathered.

The two children would play together every moment they could steal away from the grown-ups. Neither of them could remember a time before they'd been a part of each other's lives and they couldn't imagine a time would come that would tear them apart.

Even Ulriq was too young to realize that each year the hunts were bringing in less and less skins and the trading connection was growing weak. He only knew that each winter, his tribe would go out for longer and longer hunts as the animals pushed back against the demands placed upon them. The People were always careful to maintain respect for the hunt, but the ever-growing demand for hides and skins from the Russian traders pushed them to take more animals every year.

Ulriq's father was the leader of the tribe and he tried to remind the people each year of their connection to the island and the animals that shared the land. Many of the people cared less and less for their heritage and more for the fancy things the Russian traders gave to them. The growing resentment in the village against Ulriq's father was becoming apparent, even to the boy, and he feared what he didn't understand.

Soon, the sound came of their parents calling for them and they bowed their heads to hide the tears gathering in their eyes. Gently, Iliana reached out a dirty hand to trace the tear rolling down Ulriq's cheek. Angrily, he pushed it away and turned his face from her.

"Don't worry, Ulriq," Iliana spoke from behind him. "Someday, we'll grow up and get married and we won't ever have to be apart. That I can promise you."

Ulriq seized those words from the air and gathered them into his heart. He would cling to them like a lifeline in the coming days while she was far away in a distant land. The two of them were too young to realize all that stood between them and a promise. It was unheard of for a Russian princess to marry a commoner, even if he was the leader's only son. A world of difference was an obstacle even beyond the reach of their love.

Chapter Two

Kat clung to the rail of the ferry as the wretched seas tossed the boat to and fro without any concern for her lack of sea legs. She groaned as the remains of that morning's breakfast found its way overboard and sank to her knees on the filthy deck. She'd been warned the trip would be rough, but her understanding of "rough" fell far short of reality. *Traveling in a cramped plane was far better than being tossed across these relentless waves,* she thought with a groan of dismay. Leave it to her to pick the one island in the world without an airstrip.

The other teachers were sitting in the makeshift lounge making important decisions about the new school year while she struggled on deck. She knew her input wouldn't make much difference in their planning anyway. They were all returning for their second or third years here on the island. That made them the senior staff. She would get whatever position and classroom they chose not to have for themselves. It didn't seem quite fair, but it was the way the system worked.

Her vantage point from the deck gave her the privilege of being the first to see Yesterday Isle as it rose up from the waves. She stared at the barren, rocky expanse looking for something, anything to catch her eye, but nothing stood out. She didn't see any trees or plants or even any sign of human occupation. *The village must be on the other side of the island*, she thought to herself.

Suddenly, she was aware of a presence at her elbow and turned to catch sight of a quiet man with dark hair watching her. She scrambled to her feet as he began to speak.

"I'm sorry. I didn't mean to startle you. I was just wondering if you were okay," he said gently. "My name's Officer John Thompson, by the way. I serve as the peace officer in the village. My friends all call me J.T."

"Oh, hello. It's nice to meet you. I'm Kat and I'm supposed to be here to teach. Unfortunately, today I'm in the role of a student. I didn't know riding in a boat could be so...difficult."

"Ah, a landlubber I presume," J.T. said with a grim laugh. "I'd like to say don't worry, it's not always like this, but that'd be a lie and you'd soon figure it out for yourself."

"I appreciate your honesty. I have to admit that I put far more thought into the teaching part and very little into the challenges of getting here," Kat said with a weak grimace.

"Well, the good news is we're almost here as this is Yesterday Isle, well, the east side of it. You won't see the village until we round this point over to the south. The bad news is we'll have to get into the sea rafts to get to the shore. There aren't any docks or piers for us to land."

Kat looked at him with fear in her eyes and he resisted the urge to laugh. She clearly wasn't enjoying this voyage and he hurried to try and distract her.

"If you watch carefully, you will see Tomorrow Island here to the west. You're looking across the International Date Line. The two islands are only 2.4 miles apart at their closest point, but Tomorrow Island is 21 hours ahead of us, time zone wise, hence the name, Tomorrow. That island is the easternmost part of Russia. However, that doesn't make Yesterday Isle the westernmost part of the U.S. The Aleutians hold the distinction of being the westernmost and easternmost points in Alaska and by default the U.S."

"Well, aren't you just a fountain of knowledge," Marissa giggled as she slipped her arm into the crook of J.T.'s elbow. "I see you've met the new teacher. It looks like you're doing a pretty good job of impressing her with your tour guide act."

J.T. looked uncomfortable as he disengaged his arm from Marissa's grasp and took a step backwards.

"I see you've decided to come back for another year," he said a bit stiffly. "I had the impression you were considering other options...."

The unspoken question hung in the air between the three of them. Marissa turned to look out over the rail making it clear she wasn't going to answer. Jim and the other male teacher chose that moment to make their appearance on deck. Kat was embarrassed as she struggled to remember the man's name. It was clear he was Inuit and the strangeness of his name escaped her efforts to remember it.

J.T. smiled broadly at the sight of his old friend and greeted him warmly as Jim joined the two women at the rail. J.T. and the Inuit man walked off together, leaving the three of them standing at the rail in silence.

The sudden appearance of a helicopter drew their eyes upward. Kat could clearly make out someone with a camera taking pictures. They watched it fly over the village and disappear from sight at the far end.

Jim was the first to speak.

"Some rich tourists heading out to the Lodge, I bet. Well, did you give Kat the lowdown on her new job yet," he asked. "I'm sure she's dying to find out what we've decided for her."

"Not yet. I thought we'd get to the school first and have a proper meeting before handing out assignments," Marissa said with a sideways glance at Kat. "It's not really that big of a deal. The whole school only has 46 students this year. I'm really surprised they funded for four teachers."

"Maybe they were thinking ahead in order to cover themselves if someone couldn't finish out the entire year," Jim said sarcastically.

Marissa shot him a dark look before turning to go below to gather her things. She knew they were giving Kat a terrible impression even before they got to the village, but these kinds of problems were a part of the job. There was little point in trying to pretend they could all just be friends. Besides, the new girl looked like she could take care of herself. She'd definitely made an impression on J.T. He rarely spent that much time talking to new people. Shyness was his trademark, which made his role as peace officer a bit of a problem at times. Marissa wondered if Kat was going to be a problem on the small island with so few eligible men. *No worries*, she thought to herself. *I can handle a little competition.*

***

Ulriq ran down to the boats with the last of the hunting gear. His father was busy organizing the hunting parties and didn't have time to make preparations for himself. All of the men in the village would join together for the Great Hunt. It was an annual event and provided the bulk of the animals harvested each year. Individuals could continue to hunt during the dark winter months, but this single hunt was always given special attention.

The night before, the entire village had gathered for the ceremony and the great white bear, Nanuq, came to give Ulriq's father the number of animals that would be given to the men. When he revealed the number to the hunters, several of the men were angry and grumbled that the number was too low. They said the Russian traders would be disappointed with so few skins to trade.

The elders spoke and tried to remind everyone of the importance of honoring their traditions of respecting the animals, but some wouldn't listen and left the ceremony early. Ulriq caught sight of the angry glances that were cast in his father's direction. He knew his father didn't have the power to change the tally and didn't understand their anger towards him. He went to bed that night with a troubled heart.

He also worried the number of animals would be

too low, but his concerns were selfish and he dared not speak of it to anyone. Iliana's father came every year to trade for the rich pelts of the seals and otters. If there weren't enough skins to make him want to come back, Ulriq would lose his precious connection with his best friend. He'd do anything in his power to prevent this from happening. The problem was that as a young boy, his power was very limited to do anything at all.

The men rose up in the darkness of the early morning and Ulriq was one of the first to reach the boats. His father was amused at his son's eagerness and teased him about it. Ulriq turned red and turned his face away. He was sure his father didn't understand why he cared so much about the hunt and he didn't want to explain. Standing quietly, he listened as his father gave the word for the hunting party to set out for the southeast to a nearby rocky isle where the animals spent much of their day.

The men leapt into their boats and began to paddle steadily. The sea was eerily calm in the dim light and the boats moved swiftly across the water. Ulriq tried to keep pace with the men in his father's boat, but his arms were too short. His father sat behind him and watched his son's efforts proudly. *The boy had a heart for the People and would someday be a great leader*, he thought to himself.

Soon, the hunting party was in sight of the small isle and the cries of the animals carried to the men across the water. Their strokes drove deeper into the water as they hurried to arrive before their presence was noticed. With quiet movements, they landed the boats and gathered their weapons. The hunt was swift and the men worked together without a word spoken between them

Ulriq tried to keep track of his father in the activity of the hunt, but his attention was distracted and he soon lost sight of him. He wasn't allowed to join in because he'd not yet reached the age of a man. He noticed two men turn away from the others and move off from the group. His father also noticed them and followed closely behind to see where they were going.

The three men quickly disappeared around an outcropping of rocks and Ulriq lost sight of them. He stood up to see better and was relieved when the two men came back into sight. He waited for his father to reappear with them, but the man didn't come. Ulriq's stomach twisted inside him and he began to run towards the two men.

When they saw him coming, one of the men waited until he was near and hit him in the head with his club. That was the last thing Ulriq remembered when he woke up in his own hut with his mother's fearful face looming over him. His head was pounding and a bandage covered his right eye.

He wanted to ask about his father, but the look on his mother's face told him not to speak. His eyes searched the shadows behind her until the dim outline of a man came into view. He could feel this man's eyes watching and waiting to see what he would do or say. Turning his face to the wall, he closed his eyes to shut out the darkness. His father didn't come back from the hunt. Because he was too young to be the leader in his father's place, another would be chosen. It was a dark time for the People and Ulriq knew something far deeper had changed that day.

Chapter Three

Kat checked through the pile of paperwork on her desk for the third time that day and sighed. Her students clearly weren't interested in doing homework and her efforts to inspire them were falling on deaf ears. As the new teacher, her class of seven to nine year olds was far more of a challenge than she was prepared to handle. Several of the boys had learning disabilities needing special attention and the girls were only slightly better. Fortunately, there were only nine students in her class.

In a rare moment of niceness, Jim tried to explain how this particular group was the fallout of a series of particularly unqualified teachers. They started off on the wrong foot early on in their education and no one had expended the energy to set things right with them. Most of their basic skills were far below their grade level at this point. He told her it was up to her to decide where and how she would spend her efforts to deal with them. None of their parents were exactly the "PTA" type, he said with a wink.

Kat took what he said at face value. She hadn't met any of the parents from her class at the opening day gathering. The students showed up in the mornings seemingly on their own and nothing she'd sent home for a parents' signature ever came back. It was clearly up to her to step up and help these children get back on track or sit back and bide her time until the end of the year. It was an ugly choice and she wasn't the kind of person to give up on them. She had to find a way to make this work.

When it was time for the students to go home, she stood at the door and sent them off with a kind word of encouragement, or so she hoped. A couple of the boys ducked out of line and tried to avoid her. She let them slip past without comment. *Maybe, in time, they would find a way to relate to one another*, she sighed to herself.

Turning back to the table that served as her desk, Kat was startled by a male voice behind her. She jumped in surprise and scattered a pile of papers to the floor.

"I'm sorry," J.T. said as he hurried to help her gather them. "I didn't mean to frighten you. I was thinking you might be ready to see some more of the isle before it's buried in snow and ice."

Kat was actually pleased to see a friendly face and more than ready to get away from the school for a little while. There wasn't much to do on the isle, no shopping mall or theater or even any kind of restaurant. Her evenings were spent grading papers and preparing lessons. If she'd had any hope of having a social life here, that thought was dashed in the first week. None of her co-workers seemed to have any interests beyond their weak internet connection and their own classrooms. She rarely saw them beyond the meals they shared in the makeshift cafeteria.

"That sounds wonderful, J.T. I'd love to get out of this place and see something besides paperwork," she said brightly.

She couldn't help but notice the slight blush that came to his face with her words, but he just grinned and put the messy stack of papers back on her table. Taking a moment to gather her things, she watched him look around the classroom from the corner of her eye.

"How are things going with your students," he asked from the far corner of the room.

"Not as well as I'd hoped," Kat confessed as she came over to join him. "I'm having a hard time finding a way to connect with them."

"Do you mind a word of advice," J.T. asked as he studied her face.

"Not at all! In fact, I'd welcome anything that might help. I really do want to make a difference for them if I can."

"From what I've seen that doesn't work, I think your best chance is to stop talking to them and listen. Help them find their own voices and let them tell you stories. That's the way of the People, to tell stories. They really like to talk about the legends of their people, if you can get them started," he laughed, "they won't shut up."

Kat stood there for a moment and thought about his words. She was overwhelmed with the idea that he was absolutely right. She spent most of their day talking at them, and frustrated because they didn't listen. What would it hurt to turn the tables and find a way to let them talk? Her mind reeled with the possibilities contained in this simple idea. J.T.'s simple advice could change everything for her class.

"I confess I have a vested interest in your students," he said quietly. "Two of the boys are my nephews and I know they haven't been doing well in school. My sister's not much good at helping them with their studies and her husband doesn't really care. I've been trying to keep tabs on them, but my job prevents me from spending enough time with them. I'm really hoping you can help them."

Kat looked at him, but her mind was racing with new ideas so she merely nodded at this words.

"Anyway, I didn't come here to tell you how to do your job. I came to invite you to come and watch me do mine. I have to take a trip up to the Lodge and was hoping you'd like to join me. There's a good chance we'll get some moose stew out of this little excursion if we play our cards right. The cook at the Lodge is a personal friend of mine."

Kat's eyes brightened at the thought of eating something that didn't come out of a can or a freezer and she hurried to grab the rest of her things.

"You said the magic word," she laughed, "FOOD!"

J.T. laughed along with her as the two of them headed for the outside doors. Neither of them noticed Marissa standing in the shadows watching them leave together. The look on her face was anything but nice.

***

Ulriq leaned back against the rock and stared out at the icy sea. Soon the strait would be a solid sheet of ice and relatives from the other island would come to visit. It would be good to have some new faces around the village. The death of his father had caused a great rift to develop among the People and many of them were fearful. The truth of what happened was buried at the bottom of the sea with his father, but the lie left behind an ominous stench. Nothing anyone said could ever cover that up.

The two men had spread a story about his father's death. They said he'd slipped on the rocks and fallen into the sea. They hadn't been able to reach him before he slipped under the water. None of the People knew how to swim. They told everyone how Ulriq ran to help his father, but it was too late and they had to stop him for his own safety. All the people were proud to speak of Ulriq's courage to try and save his father. He knew none of this was true. He'd kept silent for his mother's sake.

The Elders were forced to choose a new leader and only one man was willing to take on that role. Everyone knew he wasn't really the right man, but he was happy to marry Ulriq's mother and take care of her and her son. That gave him honor with the People. Most of them knew he only did this because he was hoping to have a son of his own, but it didn't matter to them. His first wife and child had died during a difficult childbirth.

The man was kind to his mother and ignored Ulriq most of the time. That was enough to make the situation bearable. The boy was willing to stay quiet for his mother. Without a husband, she would have been left to fend for herself and the two of them might have starved as he was still too young to hunt. Ulriq struggled to cling to the memory of his father while everyone else tried to forget.

A sudden noise caused Ulriq to sit up in surprise. He turned to find Nanuq, the great white bear, watching him from the shadow of a nearby rock. He jumped to his feet and fought down the urge to turn and run away. Before his father's death, there was no reason to be afraid, but Ulriq knew the hunters had broken the agreement and taken more animals than the tally. No one reported the exact count, but it was clearly higher than allocated to the men. He knew there were consequences for what they had done. The problem was that without his father, there was no one who knew exactly what those consequences were going to be. Nanuq only spoke to the leader of the People.

The bear moved closer to Ulriq as he pressed himself backwards against the rock. His heart squeezed into a ball of fear and his stomach knotted. No bear had ever killed a human from the village before, but Ulriq knew the power of those claws would make quick work of him.

"I see fear in your eyes," Nanuq said quietly. "There is wisdom in being afraid."

"My father is dead," Ulriq blurted out.

"I know. There is nothing hidden in the sea that can't be found out. It is not for you to worry about, Young One. I came to tell you that justice will come for your father's death. It might not come in the way you expect or the time you hope, but I promise you it will come. Your father was a great leader and he kept the treaty of peace.

Now the treaty is broken and there is no longer

any peace between the animals and your people. There is war between us and any animal that has the chance will take the life of a human at will. You can warn the people of this, but they won't believe you. Their hearts are full of darkness and greed and they have forgotten the old ways. Soon they will lose the memory of how to speak to us and they will learn how to live with fear.

One thing I will promise you is that we will honor your father's memory. If you will remember the old ways, you and your children will continue to live under the treaty of peace. This word will stand for as long as your blood goes on in this world. If you forget and break the treaty, the word will fall with you."

Nanuq turned as if he meant to leave, but a sob came from Ulriq's throat and he turned back. Ulriq couldn't be sure, but he thought he saw a tear fall from the old bear's eye. Later, he would wonder if it was a trick of the light, but in that moment, he felt compassion and a small measure of peace. Falling to his knees, he cried until there were no more tears and when he looked up, Nanuq was gone, leaving the boy to wonder if it had all just been a dream.

Chapter Four

When they got outside, Kat looked dubiously at J.T.'s mode of transportation. She wasn't expecting much, but the ragged UTV had clearly seen better days. The battered seat was held together with layers of duct tape, peeling in more places than she could count, and the frame was wired at a couple of points with old clothes hangers. He laughed at the look on her face and jumped on to start the engine.

"Don't worry! Ole Betsy is the most reliable piece of machinery on this isle. I've fixed every part on her at least once by myself. She's never let me down."

Kat paused to consider the dichotomy of his words for a moment, but decided this was an adventure not to be missed. At the very least, she would have an interesting story to tell her students on Monday. They were all too familiar with J.T.'s antics anyway.

As they roared off down the rocky path, she leaned over to shout into his ear but only succeeded in banging her helmeted head into his. She decided this wasn't a good time for conversation and leaned back to try and enjoy the ride.

As Ole Betsy bucked and rolled down the trail, J.T. shouted greetings to everyone they passed. Kat wondered if this was his usual behavior or if he was trying to show off. She knew it would be the talk of the village before nightfall that she'd gone off with him after school. *Not that it really mattered to anyone here anyway*, she reminded herself. *I'm just another stranger passing through to them.*

After about fifteen minutes of being tossed around on the back of the vehicle, they turned a rocky corner and the Lodge came into view. Kat was overwhelmed with the beauty of the place. It had been built into a cleft of tall rocks overlooking the sea. It was hidden from the sight of the village and stood as a lonely sentry, remote and aloof.

"Welcome to Domiq," J.T. said as he shut off the UTV and waited for her to dismount.

"This place is incredible," Kat gasped as she struggled to her feet. "How...why?"

Her questions died on her lips as a movement near the front door drew her attention. J.T. quickly moved to the door to greet the woman standing there. He was one of the few villagers welcomed at this place. She reached out to hug him gently and patted him on the back.

"I see you've brought along a friend," the woman said in a melodious voice, "and a lovely one at that. Come here, Dear and let me get a closer look at you."

Kat moved over to join them and suddenly felt shy at the woman's piercing gaze. Her blue-gray eyes seemed to look right through to Kat's heart as if she were being measured. J.T. brought the uncomfortable feeling to an end with an attempt at making introductions.

"Ms. Petrova, allow me to introduce our newest teacher, Kat with a "K"..." he paused as he realized he didn't know her last name.

Both women ignored his discomfort and started to speak at the same time.

"It's nice to meet you Ms. Petrova," Kat started to say as the other woman protested.

"J.T.! How many times have I told you to call me Lana," she said.

Taking Kat by the arm, she added, "We're all friends around here and don't need to be so formal, now do we? You call me Lana and I'll call you Kat and we'll get along just fine," she said leading them inside.

J.T. followed behind the two women meekly and quietly shut the door behind them. His embarrassment faded quickly in the pleasure of bringing the two women together. He hoped they'd find some way to become friends. His concern was born out of a love and respect for the woman that had acted as a mother to him while he was growing up. It was due to her influence that he'd left the isle and attended college. His debt to this family was immeasurable.

As they were being led to the dining room, his eyes searched the rooms they passed for any signs of other guests. People often came and went from the lodge without him being aware of their visit. They came by helicopter and the helipad was on the ridge behind the building. Usually the pilots would avoid flying over the village in order not to disturb the local population. While it seemed that most of what went on out here was done in secret, J.T. was well-aware of the reasons behind all of it. He was careful to respect those reasons for Lana's sake.

"Your timing is perfect as usual J.T.," Lana said,

"you're just in time to have dinner with me."

J.T. grinned at this little ritual between them. He knew she knew he always came "just in time for dinner" and that he was always welcome at her table. He also knew there would be more than enough to eat for the three of them. There was never any chance of surprising Lana when he came for a visit. She always seemed to know he was coming, no matter the hour or the day. It was one of her mysteries that he loved about her.

True to her word, the table was already set for three as they came into the dining room and a steaming tureen sat in the middle next to a basket heaped with bread. Kat's mouth was watering before she took a seat and her eyes lit up like a child's at the sight of the food.

"I see it's been a while since you've had a good home-cooked meal," Lana said with a smile as she lifted the lid and began to ladle the stew onto their plates. "Eat up. There's plenty more where that came from."

Neither of her guests was deterred by protocol from digging into their food as the aroma wafted up to them. Rich gravy filled with chunks of moose meat and a variety of vegetables was a treat for both of them and the chewy bread only added to their pleasure. No one spoke for several minutes as the food disappeared from their plates.

Kat was the first to remember her manners as she leaned back in her chair and looked around the table. J.T. was still busy working on his second helping and Lana seemed to be picking at her original portion.

"This is wonderful," Kat sighed. "I'd given up on having anything this nice to eat until next spring."

Lana and J.T. laughed at the look on her face as she realized what she'd just said.

"Don't worry. I understand. It's hard to make anything decent with only a microwave and a small propane stove. I wouldn't survive without my kitchen or my cook. He works miracles with the simplest of ingredients," Lana said.

"So you have a staff here," Kat asked looking around the room.

"Yes and no," Lana said. "I have people here when there are guests, but much of the time, I'm here alone. The cook prepares most of what I eat in advance and freezes it for me. I just warm things up when I want to eat, though there are a few things I still like to make for myself."

Kat took in her words with a feeling of sadness. She couldn't imagine what it would be like to live alone in a place like this. *It was almost like living in exile without friends or family around*, she thought to herself.

As if Lana had discerned her thoughts, she changed the subject and asked how Kat had managed to find her way to such a remote place. The two of them listened quietly as Kat gave them a brief history of the events leading to her becoming a teacher. The fact that she'd left out a few key details didn't escape the notice of either of them. The real story, they knew, lay in the words that hadn't been spoken, but those were for her to tell when the time was right.

Once J.T. had scraped every bit of gravy from his

plate, Lana invited Kat to take a tour of her beloved Domiq. The lodge wasn't really that grand, she explained, but the story of how it came to be was amazing. It was story she loved to share with her visitors.

J.T. promised to catch up with the two women a bit later. He needed to take a look around outside and check on a few things. Without any further explanation, he disappeared out a side door leaving them alone.

Kat helped Lana clear the table and they brought the dishes into the kitchen. She was amazed to find the kitchen was an interesting blend of rustic charm and modern convenience. It was clear to her this was no ordinary woman without means. She couldn't wait to see the rest of the lodge.

**

Ulriq checked the ice every day watching for any sign that the long winter was about to release its hold on the island. The winter cold was far more brutal than anyone could remember and several of the Elders died in the course of it. Despite the excessive harvest of the great hunt, food became scarce as the hunters were forced to go farther than ever before in search of game. Several men that had gone out to hunt never came back and no traces of them were ever found.

The new leader wasn't experienced in such matters and soon found himself scorned by the other men. They came to him looking for answers and he had nothing to give them. Ulriq stayed away from his mother's hut as much as possible. There was nothing he could say that would change anything. The damage was already done.

Once the ice began to break up, Ulriq turned his attention to the horizon as he watched for the ships of the Russian traders. He wasn't really interested in the traders, but he kept that part to himself. As the days grew longer, he became more and more anxious. His heart couldn't bear the thought that Iliana wouldn't come with her father.

His fretful watch was finally rewarded with the sight of sails coming from the setting sun. He kept his post all that day and into the night as he waited for their arrival. They would wait for morning to make their way to land in the longboats. He determined, he would be the first to greet them and didn't give word to anyone.

The next morning, he stood on the shore and scanned the two ships anchored off shore, hoping to catch a glimpse of a familiar face. His heart leapt with joy when he finally saw the answer to all his prayers being helped into one of the boats. The two of them waved at one another and called out until their voices were hoarse.

Iliana was the first to be let out of the boat and in her haste dipped her skirts into the water. She ran to embrace Ulriq in a flurry of icy drops as the two of them danced in a circle of joy, much to the amusement of her parents. Others from the village had spotted the sails also and they hurried down to the shore.

Ulriq's stepfather came with his mother to meet their visitors. Unlike Ulriq's father, he spoke no Russian so the boy was pressed into service as an interpreter. Once the formalities of greetings were complete, he was then forced to relate his stepfather's version of the story of the change in leadership. Even as he spoke, Ulriq could see the questions forming in Iliana's father's eyes. Wisely, the man left them unasked and moved to the business at hand.

Explaining through the boy, Iliana's father talked of how he would like to build a dwelling place for himself and his family here on the island. There was trouble back in the mother land and he felt his family would be safer away from their home for a while. He was willing to pay for the land and would hire whomever was willing to work on the building for a fair wage.

Ulriq struggled to explain all of these matters to his stepfather as there were many words for which he had no translation. In the end, he was sure he'd made a poor job of it all, but it didn't matter. The new leader caught the basic idea that money and goods would be given to the People. His own greed was motivation enough to make him agree to whatever the Russian trader wanted from him. The entire business was settled there on the beach without any consideration from the Elders.

Iliana's father brought massive timbers to be used in building a Domiq, or lodge, for there were no large trees growing on the island. He asked Ulriq for his ideas about a suitable location. The boy brought him to a large cleft in the rocky cliffs to the north of the village. This was the place Nanuq came to speak to him after his father's death, but he didn't share that story.

As the ship's crew brought load after load of building supplies to the shore, the villagers gathered to watch this strange activity. They'd never seen such things as these massive timbers or window glass. There was even furniture and trunks full of cloth and fancy dishes. The men from the ship worked hard each day hauling things to the building site, but the villagers weren't interested in working with them. These things were not a part of their world and soon they lost interest in the entire project.

Ulriq found his own place in a cave at the back of the cleft and when he wasn't learning some new thing about building, he and Iliana spent their days together. Her parents welcomed him as if they were his family and he rarely went back to the village. In many ways, the darkness buried in his heart lifted and he teetered on the edge of manhood as his love for Iliana blossomed.

As the lodge took shape, Ulriq came to understand that Iliana and her family intended to stay on the island for the entire winter. He couldn't grasp how this would be possible for them, but he was elated with the idea. Iliana's father traded with the People and gathered all their skins and hides and a large cache of ivory carvings. He intended to take this shipload back to Russia before winter and use it to purchase the things his family would need to survive.

As the time drew nearer to winter, tensions began to grow between the Russians and the People. The new leader had no interest in friendship with Iliana's father and soon the villagers were avoiding these foreigners. Iliana's father decided it would be better to take his family back and face the trouble at home for another winter. He planned to leave a small crew of men to continue the work of building the lodge while they were away.

With a heavy heart Ulriq stood on the shore watching them leave. There were many dangers that might prevent them from returning. No one knew this better than he did, but the trip was necessary for the family's well-being. Alone and isolated from the People, they had little chance of surviving on the isle on their own.

Chapter Five

Kat studied the faces in the old portraits carefully as Lana led her up the stairs to the second floor. The stairway was a historical journey into the past as they traveled upward. The fading light made it difficult to distinguish many of the details of the faces staring out at them. Lana pointed out a few of the more storied pictures as they moved along. Losing track of the time, both women were surprised when J.T. called to them from below.

"I'm sorry, ladies. We really need to get back to the village. There's some urgent matter needing my attention," he said as they made their way back downstairs.

Kat was quiet as her mind struggled to realign itself with the present. The atmosphere of the lodge seemed to have drawn her so deeply into the past, she felt trapped there. A part of her really wanted to stay here and it was hard to say good-bye as they prepared to go.

Sensing her mood, Lana made it clear she was welcome to come back for a visit at any time. Being alone wasn't always such a good thing, she said with a laugh. She pressed Kat's hand to her cheek in an odd gesture that touched Kat's heart.

Even J.T. noted the warmth extended to the young woman and felt a flash of jealousy. He silently chided himself for being silly. It would be good for Lana to have someone around, and his duties kept him away far more than he liked. After all, that was the main reason he'd invited Kat to come out to the lodge with him.

As they rode away on the UTV, Kat couldn't help turning around to look back at the lodge. Lana stood on the porch watching them and waving good-bye. Suddenly, Kat caught sight of a face in an upstairs window, also watching. She tried to get a better view by turning around a bit more, but her efforts caused J.T. to almost lose control and drive them into a rock.

As he righted their path, he thumped her in the face with his helmeted head nearly causing her to fall off backwards. The two of them struggled to stay on as he brought the machine to a stop around a small bend which hid the lodge from their view.

"Are you okay," J.T. asked her as she shook her head.

"Yeah, sorry. I got distracted."

"By what?"

"Oh, it was nothing," she said. "I thought I saw someone looking out of an upstairs window. I'm sure it was just a reflection or something."

J.T. studied her face carefully.

"You're right. It was probably just a reflection," he said abruptly. He turned away so she couldn't see the look on his face.

**

On Monday morning, Kat's students were

strangely quiet around her. She'd taken J.T.'s advice to heart and prepared several activities to get them talking. The problem was they'd somehow lost their voices. She couldn't figure out why they were acting so odd.

The breakthrough came in the afternoon when two of the boys got into a tussle. As she pulled them apart, one of the boys pulled away from her touch. He actually seemed to be afraid of her.

"What's the matter with you two? You know there's no fighting allowed at school."

Mumbling something incoherent, both boys stared at the floor.

Kat sat down nearby as the other students gathered around them and stared at her.

"Who's going to tell me what's going on," she asked.

One of the girls finally raised her hand.

"We know you went out to that place," she said. "Did you see the pirate?"

"Domiq? The lodge, you know I went out to the lodge with J.T.," she asked them.

Slowly they nodded their heads.

"How did you....oh, I see," she hesitated. "There's no pirate. I met only an older woman living alone. Why do you think that there's a pirate?"

"Oh, we know there's a pirate living out there," one of the boys assured her. "He's a wild man with black hair and crazy eyes."

The other students nodded in agreement as they continued to stare at her.

"And you've all seen this pirate with your own

eyes?"

Their faces fell as one and she watched them carefully until one of them spoke up.

"Well, not exactly with our own eyes, but we all know someone that knows someone that's seen him," one of the students said defiantly.

Almost as a unit, they all lifted their eyes to hers and nodded again.

Her first thought was to debunk this myth with some facts, but she couldn't shake the memory of the face in the upstairs window.

"Surely if there was a pirate, Officer Thomson would know of him and take care of it," Kat said.

"He can't," one of the girls said. "You can't arrest a ghost."

Kat wanted to laugh, but the serious faces staring at her belied the urge. She scratched an imaginary itch on the back of her arm as she considered her next step. Realizing this might be an opportunity to get the students talking, she decided to approach this scientifically.

"So, you all believe there's a ghost pirate living at the lodge," she stated watching them all nod once again in agreement. "Maybe we should gather all of your evidence of this pirate and find out the truth."

The rest of the afternoon flew by as Kat listened carefully to all of the "evidence". Every student had a story to tell and while much of it was quite fanciful, the similarities were striking. There was clearly a mysterious ship that came and went under cover of darkness and a 'dark' man rarely seen. They all agreed he was up to no good and most of them were convinced he was a ghost or evil spirit.

By the time class was over for the day, all of them were sure they'd presented enough evidence to make all of their stories true. As they were leaving, Kat assured them she'd bring the matter before Officer Thomson and have him look into it. One of the boys stopped on his way out the door.

"He won't help you," he said. "The pirate is his brother."

Kat stared after him long after he'd left wondering what he meant.

Chapter Six

After a rough night dreaming of pirates and faces in distant windows, Kat was late getting to her classroom the next morning. She was surprised to hear angry voices coming from the room as she approached. When she came in, two women glared at her from the back of the room. Jim was trying to make some kind of explanation to them, but stopped at her entrance. Basically, he shrugged his shoulders and took a step back as the women stepped towards her.

"You shouldn't be telling our kids ghost stories," the first woman growled at her. "My girl was up all night having nightmares!"

"What kind of a teacher are you," the other woman chimed in.

Kat didn't know what to say. Her first thought was that she hadn't told any ghost stories, but knew that wasn't going to help her. She couldn't help but notice Jim slipping out of the room. A few of the students were sitting in their desks watching her carefully.

"Good morning, Kat," came a cheery voice from behind her.

Everyone turned to see Officer Thomson standing in the doorway. He greeted the two women and invited them to step outside with him. They glared at Kat as they followed him out. She could hear them expressing their displeasure all the way down the hall. Making her way to the front of the room, she took a deep breath and struggled to calm herself. *Maybe it would be better to stick to reading, writing and arithmetic*, she thought to herself. *There's no point in getting the parents mad at me.*

Hoping to get the day off to a better start, Kat pulled out an art project she'd selected and set the children to drawing animals. No one talked about ghosts or pirates and by the time lunch came around, she was hoping to let the matter rest. Most of the students had finished their pictures so Kat began hanging them up around the classroom. Each student would point to their drawing proudly after she'd pinned it up. She wasn't surprised to see that many of them had drawn polar bears.

Her afternoon activity was to have the children write a story about the animal in their drawing. She moved among them quietly helping with word questions and spelling. Many of them managed to come up with nearly a page of writing by the end of the class. The rest of the afternoon was intended to allow the students to come up and read or tell their stories. Feeling confident that none of the stories would bring out pirates or ghosts, Kat took a seat at the back of the class and prepared to listen. The first volunteer went to stand under her picture of a polar bear.

"This is Nanuq, the great white bear," the little girl began. "A long time ago, the People were friends with Nanuq and they could talk to him…"

"That's not true," one of the boys shouted. "You're

a liar!"

"It is so," the little girl shouted back. "My grandmother told me because her grandmother told her!"

Before Kat could gain control, all of the students were shouting their agreement or opposition to the story and the little girl began to cry. Trying to quiet them, Kat wasn't surprised to see Jim poke his head in the door with a sour look on his face. He took a quick look at the situation and retreated. *Thanks for the help,* Kat thought. Holding her hand over her mouth in an exaggerated gesture, she looked at each student in turn until they fell silent.

"Everyone take out your library book and read silently," she said guiding the girl back to her desk.

"It is true," the little girl whispered as Kat handed her a tissue.

Kat just nodded.

***

Winter came that year with a vengeance and the People struggled with the extreme cold it brought to the isle far too early. As they made preparations for the Great Hunt, many of them feared the strange conditions would prevent them from going out. On the evening before the Hunt, all of the People gathered for the ceremony, as was their custom.

Ulriq's stepfather was very anxious as they waited for Nanuq to make his appearance. He didn't know how to talk to the Great White Bear, but he couldn't say that to the People. They would reject him as their leader. He tried to put on a bold face and spoke loudly to everyone around him to hide his fear.

The hour was very late when the People began to accept that Nanuq wasn't going to come to the ceremony. Some of them suggested he had died and others whispered words they didn't dare speak aloud. Many of the men gave voice to the idea of canceling the Great Hunt, but this would put all of the People at risk of starving during the long winter.

Finally the Elders gave the decree the hunters would use the same tally as last year. No mention was made of the fact that the hunters had broken the tally agreement. Some words were better left unspoken.

Ulriq was up early the next morning to prepare for his first hunt without his father. This year, he was old enough to participate with the other men, but his heart was heavy with dark memories. He took no pleasure in his preparations as he labored under ominous gray skies. The men were silent as they paddled their boats to the hunting place.

As the rocky isle came into sight, the men were surprised to see several polar bears lined up along the shore. The bears appeared ready to rebuff them from landing on the isle. As the boats drew closer, the polar bears stood up to their full height and roared in anger at the men. All of the men reacted in fear at this strange behavior and no one was willing to try and land their boat. Without a word, the boats turned around and headed back home.

When they reached the isle, all of the men gathered around the leader to see what he would say about this. He was silent in the face of their fear and anger and had no plan for them. Finally, one man suggested that they might try again tomorrow and see if the bears were still there. Grumbling among themselves, they headed back to their huts hoping to see better luck the next day.

Ulriq lay in his sleeping spot that night and listened to the wind howling outside. It carried the sound of angry voices into his dreams and he slept badly. The next morning the winds continued and all through that day and the next. There was no chance the boats could leave the isle. No one could remember a time when there'd been no Great Hunt. It was going to be a very hard winter if they had no food.

Several weeks passed before Ulriq could make the short trip up to the lodge to check on the progress of the men staying there. They were busy with their work and unaware of the situation in the village. The boy was their only contact with the People. He didn't tell them what had happened on the Great Hunt. They probably wouldn't have believed him anyway.

Chapter Seven

Kat wasn't too excited with her progress in getting the students to talk. It wasn't that the students weren't talking, but they only wanted to talk about things they weren't allowed to talk about at home. She didn't understand the cultural barriers or the issues her students faced. This created conflicts between the students and problems with the parents.

By the end of the first week of this experiment, Kat was inclined to go back to the old model of her talking and the students listening. It was far easier even if it wasn't very effective. The only bright spot in the week was J.T. bringing her a note from Lana inviting her to Domiq for the weekend. She read it while he waited for her answer and gave him a hearty reply fueled by her own growing loneliness. Having something ahead of her caused the rest of the week fly by and soon she was clearing her desk while she waited for J.T.

The sound of angry voices in the hall drew her to the door of her classroom. Peeking out, she caught sight of Marissa confronting J.T. Missing the context, Kat wasn't sure of the point of the argument and she didn't want to be caught eavesdropping so she retreated to her desk. The voices seemed to fade as she waited for J.T. to appear. The silence nearly drew her back to the hall, but J.T.'s sudden appearance in the doorway stopped her midway. His red face said far more than his simple question of "are you ready" and she only nodded her head. Grabbing her bag, she hurried to follow after him as he turned and left without another word.

They rode out to the lodge without speaking and J.T. didn't bother to smile and wave at anyone they passed along the way. He just stared straight ahead and Kat felt the tension in his back as she struggled to hold on while giving him some space. It was clear the exchange with Marissa was still very much on his mind by the time they arrived.

As Kat dismounted, J.T. turned to her with a terse promise to be back for her on Sunday. She barely had a chance to reply before he drove away leaving her standing there. She stood there watching him drive away, lost in thought.

"Are you planning on standing there much longer," Lana called in a friendly voice from the front door. "I'm not wearing a coat and its cold out here."

She laughed as Kat turned a startled face towards her and hurried towards the door.

"I'm sorry," Kat said. "I....J.T..., well, he seemed upset."

"Hmm," was all Lana said as she drew Kat inside the warmth of the lodge.

The lodge was filled with the sweet aroma of baking and Kat's stomach rumbled as she pulled off her heavy coat.

"Something smells heavenly," she breathed with a sigh of delight.

"Ah, yes! We couldn't have a visit without something special to eat," Lana smiled at her guest.

"Besides, it's a trick of the trade to make one's guests feel welcome."

The two women made their way to the kitchen.

"I'm so pleased you accepted my invitation. Your visit has really given me something to look forward to this weekend."

"Oh, me too! I've had such a week and your invite is the only thing that got me through it," Kat said.

"Let's sit down here in the kitchen while I finish baking these cookies and you can tell me about it. I don't know much about teaching, but I have learned some things in my lifetime that might help," Lana said with a smile.

They spent the next two hours as Kat poured out the challenges she faced in her classroom. The warmth and bright lights of the kitchen made stories of pirates and talking bears seem silly so she left most of that out. Lana was a good listener and Kat found her concerns slipping away. The problems at school weren't anywhere near as interesting as the woman sitting before her.

"That's enough about my silly problems," Kat laughed. "I'd rather hear your stories. I've thought about little else since J.T. brought me here. It's your turn to talk my ear off."

Lana laughed as she considered where to begin.

"I'm afraid it's a very long story and you'll get bored with me."

"We've got all winter and I highly doubt you could bore me with anything. These cookies alone are worth the trip!" Kat grinned as she reached for her third one.

"Then I think we should start at the beginning,"

Lana mused. "I also think a story's better with pictures so let's go upstairs, shall we?"

Grabbing Kat's overnight bag on the way, the two women headed upstairs. Lana paused in front of a very old picture and pointed the couple out to Kat.

"The story begins here," she said. "Allow me to introduce my great-grandfather, Ulriq and my great-grandmother, Iliana. I'm actually named after her. Lana's just a nickname my brother gave me a long time ago."

Kat stared at the picture of the unsmiling faces staring back at her. The strange sensation of being drawn back into the past, their present, caused her to wobble a bit. Lana reached out a hand to steady her.

"You feel them too, don't you," Lana asked quietly.

Kat pulled her eyes from the picture to stare at Lana.

"You look so much like her," was all she managed to say.

***

The winter was the hardest the People could ever remember. Without the Great Hunt, they were forced to go out seeking food almost every day. Many days, the winds and the cold made hunting or fishing impossible. It wasn't too long before hunger began to claim the weakest, and the darkest months were still ahead of them.

Ulriq divided his time between the men at the lodge and fishing for his mother. The workmen had a sufficient supply of foodstuffs in storage and weren't affected by the lack of meat. They were used to a diet of hardtack and dried food. No one in the village realized or even cared to know how the foreigners were faring out beyond the edge of their small community. They had too much trouble at home.

Ulriq's fishing skills weren't especially noteworthy, but he always managed to bring home two or three fish on each trip. He suspected the bears were somehow helping him by herding fish towards him underneath the ice, but he could never prove this with any real confidence. He never saw anything more than fleeting shadows in the darkness of the icy water. It was enough to know that he was a part of something greater than himself.

His mother tried to help out the Elders and some of the other mothers by sharing what she could, but there was never enough for everyone. When some of the men learned there was food in the leader's house, they became angry towards him and evil rumors went around about the family. They were forced to be more and more secretive as the People grew more desperate. Ulriq learned to come and go from the village under the cover of darkness or storms. Fear was taking hold of everyone and the new leader was powerless to contain it.

When the dark time came, fewer men were willing to go out to hunt or fish. The People from the neighboring island came to visit relatives and were horrified at what they found. There was plenty of food on their island and it didn't take much to convince the others to go back with them. One family at a time, they began to migrate over the ice to the larger western island.

As the huts slowly emptied out, the few fish Ulriq brought home went further and the ugly rumors changed to quietly whispered words of gratitude. Though he was barely a man, some of the People began to talk of how he was their true leader. These words angered his stepfather and soon Ulriq found himself unwelcome in his own home. His mother was powerless against her husband's jealousy and she warned her son to stay away for his own safety. He stayed at his cave behind the lodge for longer periods of time, coming only to the village to bring his mother food. The winter was a long and lonely time and only his thoughts of his beloved Iliana sustained him. He dreamed of her return every night.

Chapter Eight

Lana pulled a worn journal from a trunk in the sitting room and stroked the cover gently. Kat could feel her mind being drawn into the past as the room cloaked them in silence. Only the sound of the wind swirling around the corners of the house came to her ears. The old house stood as solid as a fortress against the onslaught of the cold outside, as it had done for generations. *It had been built to withstand a thousand winters far worse than this,* Kat thought to herself.

"This is my great-grandmother, Iliana's journal," Lana began. "The sad thing is that it's in Russian and I never learned to read it though I can understand the spoken language. The words have been lost to my family because of this."

"How odd," Kat said in surprise, "because I can read Russian. My first name's actually Katerina and my mother's family were second generation Russian immigrants. I became very interested in my family genealogy when I was young and my babushka taught me many things about the motherland. I'm not very good, but I'm willing to try."

Lana's eyes lit up at this revelation and she passed the cherished book to her guest.

"I would be greatly honored if you would do that for me," she said with tears in her eyes.

Holding the treasure on her lap, Kat closed her eyes for a moment and formed a picture of her beloved babushka in her mind. The old woman had seemed ancient to Kat with her wrinkled skin and weathered face. She'd tried to keep the connection to their roots alive in the family, but the young generation only wanted to know about the present or the future. The past held little interest to all of them, except for Kat. She listened again and again to the old stories and legends until they were as much a part of her as the fairy tales shown on TV or read to her from books.

The fire in her blood lit by those stories called for her to make a trip to visit Russia when she finished college. Despite all that her grandmother had told her, present day Russia bore little resemblance to the memories she held in her heart. The death of her grandmother left a void in her life and her trip put a lock on the door to the past. There was no place to go back to in the motherland anymore.

Carefully, Kat lifted the cover of the journal and peeked inside at the faded writing. The delicate letters at first confused her as her mind struggled to make sense of the unfamiliar characters. This had clearly been written before the time of Kat's grandmother. It took her several minutes to work out the words of the first sentence.

Looking up at Lana with a sad face, she pursed her lips in frustration.

"This is going to take some time," Kat said. "I'm not as familiar with the older forms."

Lana shrugged.

"That's okay. Like you said, we've got all winter."

The two women laughed at that and Kat turned back to the text. She began to read slowly in broken Russian as the present world faded and Iliana's words drew them to another time. Neither of the women noticed the presence leaning against the doorway of the room taking in the words along with them. It was as if they were alone in another world.

***

If winter had come swiftly to the isle, the haste with which it departed was equally as sudden. In a normal year, the ice in the strait took weeks to break up. The People would stop everything to watch for the first cracks to appear and begin to count the days until it was gone. This strange year brought danger as the ice shifted and collapsed upon itself in ways never seen in the past.

Two men manning a fishing hole lost their lives when a sudden upheaval cast them into the sea. This served as a warning to the others to stay ashore until the ice floes were driven away by the strong ocean currents or risk losing their own lives. The hunger and the frustration of the People continued to grow and their leader was powerless to help them. Even worse, the desperate winter without the Great Hunt left the People with nothing to trade for food when the ships would come from afar seeking hides and skins. There was great fear in the village that there would be no relief from their suffering.

The builders at the lodge were also growing

anxious as their own supplies dwindled and their patience wore thin. A couple of the men had families back on the mainland and hoped to return to them. The others had grown tired of the isolation and seemingly endless cold. The majority of their work on the lodge was complete, leaving them with too much time on their hands.

Ulriq withdrew from them as squabbles and fights broke out over trivial matters. He resumed his post on the bluffs to watch for the return of his beloved and her family. It was a difficult wait as there were no guarantees he could hold out, only this burning hope fueled by his love. His one relief was sleep and even there he dreamed of sailing ships and great white bears.

When the water was free of the ice, the first birds flew in on a warm breeze bringing life back to the village. As they gathered eggs, the People began to realize how much had been lost to them. More than half of the population was dead or gone and the few left were weak and sickly. The empty, broken-down huts outnumbered the homes of the others and many doors swung brokenly in the wind with no one to fasten them shut anymore.

When the first sails appeared on the horizon, Ulriq spent nearly an hour trying to convince himself that he'd simply imagined them. He ran back and forth along the shore changing the angle of his view until he was worn out. Casting himself to the ground, he leaned against a rock and stared out over the water until his eyes were blurred.

Finally, he fell asleep where he lay and dreamed

that Nanuq had come down to the shore to wait with him. The great white bear talked to him of many things, but when he awoke, he remembered nothing that was said. He felt a great peace had somehow settled inside of him and all of his fears for the future were washed away.

Wiping the sleep from his eyes, he turned his gaze out over the waters. His heart leapt with joy to see a ship drawing nearer to the isle. He could make out some activity on the deck as they prepared to launch the longboats. He ran to tell the workmen at the lodge of the ship and they hurried with him to the landing place. The People from the village did not join with them in the greeting this time.

He clearly saw Iliana and her mother being helped into the first boat with her father but somehow he felt strangely shy and didn't return her waves. His hand trembled at his side, but having suffered so much, the boy he had been no longer waited for her. Ulriq knew he had crossed over and left his childhood behind in the harsh winter. He sensed this would change things between him and Iliana. He only hoped the change would be for the better as his love caused his heart to beat strangely within him.

Watching the young woman climbing from the boat, he realized she too had grown up and left her childhood behind. He wondered at the world she'd left and what she'd had to face in the many months they'd been apart. He knew little of political unrest or the complexities of revolution. Turning to look at her parents, it was clear the winter hadn't been kind to them either. Both of them looked worn and tired beyond the trials of their journey.

They came together shyly and acted for the moment almost as if they were strangers. Iliana's father broke the tension between them by grabbing Ulriq and embracing him heartily as an old friend. Soon the four of them were laughing and talking as they tried to catch up with their news. Ulriq spoke proudly of the work done during the winter on the lodge as the men unloaded supplies from the ship.

Leaving his men to their tasks, Iliana's father was anxious to see the lodge, so the four of them began the walk through the village. They fell silent as the family saw the empty huts and the hollow faces of the People watching them from their doorways. At first, they'd called out greetings, but their words were met with silence and downcast faces.

As they reached the end of the village, Ulriq saw tears in the eyes of Iliana and her mother. Her father quietly asked him what had happened over the winter. The explanation was beyond words and Ulriq simply shook his head. It was enough to see the empty faces to know the winter was very bad. They walked on without speaking.

Coming around the final outcropping of rock brought the lodge into view. Iliana gasped at the sight and Ulriq caught up her hand. The two of them began to run the final distance leaving her parents to follow. The workmen had wasted little time using every spare minute to carve intricate details around the main doorway and the windows. The entire structure was closely enjoined with the surrounding rock leaving the impression it was somehow a part of the isle.

The windows facing west over the strait sparkled in the sunlight. An air of peace blanketed the entire house, drawing them inside. Carved banisters graced the curving stairway inside the main entrance and the massive log walls muffled the sound of the ocean nearby into a quiet murmur. The four of them moved quietly from room to room trying to take it all in at once.

Even though Ulriq had spent the winter watching the workmen at their work, he felt as if he was seeing it all for the first time himself as he considered it through their eyes. *This is a home worthy of a princess,* he thought to himself.

Chapter Nine

Kat woke up the next morning with a start. The sun was shining through a small gap in the heavy drapes. Stretching herself in the soft sheets, she enjoyed the comfort of a real bed. The sturdy cot in her room left little room to turn over, let alone stretch. Her thoughts drifted back to the journal and the words of last night. She'd read until her yawning made them realize the late hour.

Just before she'd slipped into bed, she'd gone to the window and looked out over the strait. Much to her surprise, she saw lights bobbing up and down out on the water right in front of the lodge. As she watched, the lights suddenly disappeared from her view. She stared out at the darkness for half an hour before she'd decided she must have imagined it and went to bed.

As her stomach gave a groan, she realized that a wonderful aroma had wafted into the room while she'd slept. It was time to go in search of breakfast. Without thinking, she slipped out of bed and ran a quick brush through her hair.

Hurrying downstairs in her pajamas, she turned the corner to head for the kitchen and ran straight into a man carrying a heavy tote sack. Her momentum and his heavy load caused the two of them to stumble in surprise. He dropped the heavy sack with a crash, knocking a vase off a nearby table. She bounced off the wall and landed in a heap at his feet.

"Oh my," Lana said as she ran from the kitchen to help Kat to her feet. "Are you all right?"

"Yes. Yes, I think so," Kat said a bit shakily as she eyed the stranger warily. "I didn't realize there was anyone else here in the house with us."

Suddenly aware that she was wearing her pajamas, her face turned red and she quickly turned to head back upstairs. The strange man was down on his knees picking up the broken pieces of the vase with his face turned away from her. Lana watched her retreat and then turned to help with the mess. The two of them worked quietly to set things back in order.

Kat sat down on the bed to gather her wits. She hadn't expected there to be anyone else at the lodge this weekend. It was a stupid assumption on her part as guests came and went without anyone's knowledge in the village, as far as she knew. Shaking off her embarrassment, she hurried to get dressed. Checking her image in the mirror, she was startled by a knock at the door.

"Kat, can I come in," Lana called.

"Of course," Kat said as she opened the door.

"I'm sorry," both women said at the same time and laughed.

"It's nothing to be sorry about, my dear," Lana said, "you couldn't have known there was someone in the house besides us. Even I was surprised to find my son at home this morning. He comes and goes as he pleases without warning. I've gotten used to it."

"So that was your son downstairs that I mowed down in the hallway?"

"Yes, and don't worry. He's none the worse for the wear. He was more concerned about you since you landed on the floor," Lana laughed.

"No, I'm fine. I've taken worse tumbles playing games with my students."

"Well, why don't you come downstairs? Breakfast is ready and I can introduce you two properly," Lana said taking Kat by the arm.

The two of them headed for the kitchen arm in arm. Kat was glad for the company as she felt unnaturally shy after their abrupt collision. Finding him at the table calmly buttering a scone brought a sense of relief to her. He appeared quite ordinary in the bright lights of the kitchen. *Not at all like one would imagine a pirate to look like,* Kat laughed to herself as she sat down.

"I always thought I was the biggest fan of my mother's cooking, but I can see that I've been out matched," the stranger said with a grin.

As the man turned to look at Kat, her breath caught in her throat as their eyes met. His attempt at humor was lost on her as she found herself torn between his dark eyes and the ragged scar that marred the right side of his face. Running from his hairline to just below his ear, it was easy to imagine the slash of a sword in the hands of a pirate.

"Now you promised to be nice, Alexei," Lana scolded. "Running over our guests in the hallway isn't how you were raised, nor were you ever allowed to tease."

Kat busied herself with sitting down at the table, giving herself time to gather her wits. As Lana attempted to make polite introductions, Alexei went back to buttering his scone. He mumbled something that passed for an acknowledgment and began eating without another word. His mother made a face at him and gave Kat a wan smile.

"I fear I've raised a barbarian," she said as she watched her son. "Here, dear, have something to eat before my son finishes off the scones," she laughed as she handed Kat the platter.

Kat spent the next few minutes filling her plate with scrambled eggs and hash browns, as her stomach urged her on. She couldn't resist taking a bit of each before taking the next serving dish, much to the amusement of her hosts. Even Alexei had stopped eating to watch her performance. Feeling his eyes upon her, Kat looked up to find them both watching her with grins on their faces. Turning red to the roots of her hair, she froze in the middle of a large bite of her scone, leaving butter running down the side of her mouth to drip from her chin.

Gently, Alexei reached out with a napkin to catch it before it landed on her shirt.

"Slow down there, little one," he said quietly, "I promise I won't eat all of the scones."

The sound of Lana pushing her chair back broke the moment as she assured them there were plenty of scones, and headed over to the stove to prove it. Kat couldn't help but notice a slightly annoyed look on her face as she turned away. She wondered if the look was on her account or his, but Lana came back with her usual smile leaving Kat to think she'd misread the woman. She reminded herself this was only her second visit to Domiq and she really hadn't gotten to know Lana yet.

Breakfast passed with Lana doing most of the talking as she related the story from her great-grandmother's journal to her son. Alexei was clearly as interested in the tale as his mother and asked several questions. Like his mother, he spoke some Russian but never learned to read the language for himself. Kat was surprised when he asked her to continue the reading there at the kitchen table while he washed the breakfast dishes.

Lana gave her a wink as she said, "I must have done something right, eh?"

Kat was happy to oblige as she was just as intrigued with the tale as them.

**

Conditions in the village and the lack of furs and pelts for trading deeply concerned Iliana's parents. Her father was forced to sail beyond the islands to the mainland to trade with the people there. Leaving his wife and daughter on the isle was a difficult decision, but as this was meant to be their new home, he felt it would be okay. He charged Ulriq with their care and sailed away. The three of them stood on the shore and watched until the sails disappeared from their sight. Without a word, they turned and headed to Domiq with heavy hearts.

The summer days passed pleasantly enough as Iliana's mother left them to amuse themselves as she busied herself setting her new home in order. When they weren't called upon to move some piece of furniture or admire her latest handiwork, they explored the caves and the isle from one end to the other.

Iliana took it upon herself to teach Ulriq how to read and write, though he had little interest. He was willing to do whatever she asked just to be with her. Each day they'd spend some time looking at the few books her father had brought along. The one that held their interest was an atlas with maps of the entire world. Seeing their tiny isle as a dot compared to the land Iliana called home was hard for Ulriq to comprehend. He'd never left his home, not even to visit the neighboring island within sight. She would trace out the path on the map to her faraway home over and over again until he could see it with his eyes closed. How that picture related to the reality of land and sea, he couldn't even begin to understand.

When her father returned with a ship laden with furs and pelts from the mainland, he found himself facing another decision. He needed to return to the motherland to fulfill his contracts and buy the supplies they'd need for the winter. With a plan in place to return for the winter, the question was whether or not he would bring his family with him or leave them once again. Deciding the risk was too great that he might not make the return trip in time before winter set in, he thought it best to take them with him.

Iliana was heartbroken to leave Ulriq behind again and pleaded with her father to allow Ulriq to come with them. It didn't take much to convince her parents as they made preparations to leave and Ulriq found himself in the longboat heading away from home for the first time in his life. His mother was happy for him and his stepfather simply didn't care. The choice for him was simple, he would go wherever Iliana bade him to go, without hesitation.

Chapter Ten

Kat struggled to make out the faded letters on the brittle pages of the journal. *Time was doing its best to erase the history of this family right before their eyes,* she thought. Reading slowly and carefully, the three of them were caught up and drawn back into a Russia that no longer existed.

Iliana wrote each day of the strange, new world she was sharing with her beloved Ulriq. Everything was new for him, the ship, the food, and the crowds of people everywhere they traveled. He quickly became overwhelmed with all of it and fell ill for several weeks. Iliana stayed at his side the entire time as she nursed him back to health.

Her parents questioned the wisdom of bringing him away from his home as they feared for his life. It wouldn't do to go back to the isle to report his death to his parents. They would never be able to understand what had happened to him. The consequences might even cost them Domiq and their chance for a new life there on the isle. His recovery was cause for a great celebration.

Kat felt the relief in the room as she read of the party thrown in his honor. It almost made her laugh as they had the evidence on the wall upstairs of his recovery, yet Iliana's worry had reached out from the past and caught them all in its grip. The power of her words transcended time for all of them.

The family began to make preparations to return to the isle and Iliana filled her journal with lists of things to take and other stuff to give away to friends or neighbors. It appeared the decision was made to make this their final move. Their house in Ayan was going to be transferred to a brother or a cousin, according to what Kat could make out.

A large gap in the daily entries caused her to pause in her reading.

"It appears that Iliana stopped writing for several weeks here," Kat said looking up at the others. "This next entry records the arrest of her father. She doesn't explain why. Her mother went to protest to the authorities and didn't come home again. She believes they are dead."

"Many of the aristocrats were caught up in a rebellion against the ruling classes during that time in the history of Russia," Lana said sadly. "It's a very dark time. Perhaps their deaths were related to that."

"What does she write of next," Alexei asked hovering over the journal. "Obviously she somehow manages to escape."

"Maybe Kat would like to take a break," Lana suggested. "She's been reading for nearly an hour."

"Actually, I could do with some fresh air," Kat said. "I'd like to take a little walk outside and enjoy the sunlight."

"That sounds like a good idea," Lana agreed, "but I insist that Alexei must come with you. There are....hazards outside for someone unfamiliar with the area. I think I'll lay down for a short nap while you're gone."

Both Kat and Alexei looked at Lana, but she didn't say anything more. They stood at the same time and headed for the door. Nearly colliding again, Alexei stopped short and bowed to her.

"After you," he said gallantly as he waited for her to pass.

She made a face at him as she left the kitchen. He simply smiled.

***

Ulriq felt helpless in the face of their situation. The sudden arrest of Iliana's father came just as they were getting ready to leave Ayan. He had no warning that his name was on the list of those to be rounded up by the authorities. Her mother went to the officials trying to find his location and the charges brought against him. She was warned to stay away, but she went again the next day.

When she didn't come home, Iliana went to talk to her uncle. He wouldn't open the door to his niece and warned her to leave the city as fast as she could go. He was planning to leave that very night and wouldn't be coming back. There was no room in his escape plan for Iliana and Ulriq. They were on their own.

Iliana tried to explain the danger to Ulriq, but he knew nothing of such things. The one part of the situation he did understand was that fathers sometimes died under strange circumstances. With this thought in mind, he knew it was up to him to protect his beloved and get her home to the isle. He knew they would have to travel a very long way up the coast before they could cross the ice. Without her father's ship, it would take weeks to walk that far.

Together, they gathered all the supplies they could carry into a small cart pulled by a very large horse and waited until it was dark to leave. Some family portraits and her mother's jewelry fit into a small chest at the very bottom of their stash. It was all she had left of her family and Ulriq didn't protest when she packed her treasures. They filled the rest of the space with food and winter clothing, knowing there would be little chance to find anything along the way.

Once they got beyond the town and the few outlying houses, Ulriq felt his confidence grow that he could get them home. They were both strong and healthy and he was a hunter. At first, Iliana laughed as he strutted about taking charge of making fires and setting up their campsites, but soon she too felt confident in his care. She believed he would do everything in his power to keep her safe.

One morning, Ulriq woke up first. Iliana was curled up against him and her warmth was making him feel very strange towards her. He tried to get up without waking her, but the cold air slipped in and brought her around.

"Where are you going," she asked drowsily.

He didn't answer but quickly turned away from her and headed out of their camp.

Iliana sat up and looked after him wondering at his behavior. He wasn't inclined to be so abrupt with her. She scanned the area for any sign of a disturbance, but nothing seemed to be wrong. The horse was quietly munching on a bit of shrubbery and the fire still gave off a bit of heat from the rocks surrounding it. Shrugging her shoulders, she got up and rolled up their bedding before looking through their foodstuffs for breakfast. Ulriq came back while she was foraging through their packs and sat down on the far side of the fire.

"Iliana," he said quietly, "do you love me?"

"You know I love you. I've loved you for as long as I can remember."

"Iliana, do you remember when you said we'd be married someday and we'd never have to be apart ever again?"

Busy scraping some mold off a bit of cheese, she didn't look up at him, but just nodded her head.

"I think this is that 'someday'", Ulriq said firmly.

As his words sunk into her, she froze and stared down at her hands.

"Ulriq, how can we get married," she finally asked. "We're all alone out here."

"That's true, and I think that's why we need to get married."

Iliana sat there for a long time without speaking. Thoughts of weddings and churches ran through her head followed by flowing dresses and flowers, lots of flowers. She'd only been to a couple of weddings in her short life, but the images were burned into her brain. Nothing out here in this wilderness lent itself to such an event. There wasn't even a priest anywhere to speak all the words needed to be spoken. Tears came to her eyes as she considered this matter. *How shall I get married without my Mama and my Papa*, she thought to herself.

Ulriq, seeing tears in the eyes of his beloved, nearly started to cry himself. His greatest fear in this moment was that she didn't want to marry him now. He didn't know how he would go on knowing she didn't love him enough to be his wife.

"If you don't want to marry me..." he began and then choked on the rest of his words.

Jumping up and coming over to his side, Iliana knelt down beside him.

"It's not that I don't want to marry you," she said. "This just isn't how I thought our wedding would be. I don't know how we can marry out here."

"I think we have to do it the way my People get married," Ulriq said looking at her with hope in his eyes. "We can make our own marriage anyway you want. We just need to say the words of joining to each other in front of a witness. We can stand in front of the horse!"

Iliana began to giggle at the thought of being married by a horse. Maybe Ulriq was right and they could make their own wedding. There was no one to judge them out here anyway. She jumped up and looked around their campsite. Seeing some tiny flowers, she ran to gather a small bunch of them.

Ulriq was more interested in the preparations she'd started for breakfast and turned his attention to finding something to eat.

"What are you doing," she asked. "I thought we were going to get married."

"I think I'd like to have something to eat first. I don't have the strength to make a wedding on an empty stomach," he said as he grinned at her.

"You're right! Let's eat and then we'll get married," she said plopping down next to him. "It's not like we need to be in a big hurry."

With the matter settled, the two of them nibbled at the last of the cheese and some stale bread. They both knew the food they'd brought along wasn't going to last much longer. Soon Ulriq would have to try to hunt. The problem for him was that there was nothing in this land he was familiar with hunting. It would take working together to overcome this challenge. The isle seemed very far away to both of them.

Chapter Eleven

That evening, the three of them gathered in the sitting room with Iliana's journal and a plate of Lana's cookies. Picking up where she'd left off, Kat began to read quietly as the wind blew outside. As before, the simple words drew them into the past and their present time slipped away.

She'd been reading for a couple of hours when a sound at the front door caused them all to look up. Alexei went to see to the matter as the two women waited for his return.

"I'm sorry, Mother," Alexei said, "something's come up and I have to go. Please excuse me, Kat, and thanks for the reading." With those words he was gone, leaving the two of them staring at an empty doorway.

"I think we should call it an evening," Lana said as she stood up. "It's been wonderful hearing you read, but I'm feeling a bit tired. You're free to stay up and explore the house if you'd like. I'll see you in the morning."

Before Kat could say anything, Lana was gone and she was left in the sitting room alone. Feeling a bit strange at the suddenness of her hosts' departures, Kat decided to go to her room and turn in early. She hated leaving Iliana and Ulriq in the middle of their perilous journey, but reading the journal alone almost seemed like spying somehow. The warmth of her room and the comfort of the soft bed quickly lulled her to sleep and soon she was dreaming of two people alone in the vast wilderness with no one to care if they lived or died.

***

As the winter snows grew deeper, the little cart became more of a hindrance than a help to them. Iliana wanted to leave the cart behind and take the horse, but Ulriq knew the horse would be of little use to them crossing the ice. He spent some days studying the cart before taking a large rock and tearing it apart.

Iliana sat on a log and watched him quietly as he worked. She was delighted to see his handiwork in the end. He'd turned their little cart into a small sled that was easier for the horse to pull through the snow. When the horse was no longer able to do so, they would be able to pull the small conveyance with their few belongings easily across the ice.

They'd tried to stay within sight of the ocean for as much of their journey as possible, but some of the larger rivers had forced them inland a few times to find places to cross. As the land settled in under a blanket of ice and snow, it was easier to avoid these detours and soon they found themselves nearing the last barrier to their destination.

The Bering Sea ice was treacherous to cross in the coldest of winters. This winter seemed milder than usual and Ulriq feared the ice may not have fully closed the gap between this land and the islands. They really had no choice but to go forward on faith. There was nothing left behind them and the only home they knew was Domiq where they would be safe. Wisely, he kept his fears to himself. There was no point in putting more on Iliana than she could bear, he thought.

Reaching the end of the land, they stood together looking out over the ice. Their destination lay beyond their sight at this point. Ulriq didn't know how long it would take them to cross, nor was he even sure this was possible. The People talked of others who'd made this journey long ago, but all anyone really knew was that it was a long and hazardous trek.

Using their last campsite as a place to gather a cache of firewood and snare a few rabbits, Ulriq watched the ice every day for some sign it was safe to cross. Iliana sorted through their packs and used her time to find a place for everything on the sled. They both knew it was time to say good-bye to the horse as it had a better chance of surviving back on land.

Removing the straps and ropes from the horse, Ulriq quietly whispered their thanks and some final words of advice into the horse's ear before turning him loose. With a last look back, the horse gave out a whinny and a snort before heading back at a trot the way they'd come. The two of them stood there holding hands as they watched their friend depart. He was the last witness to their existence in the land.

That night, they lay together under the stars and watched the Great Lights dance their fire across the sky. Ulriq believed this was the sign he'd been waiting for and determined they would begin crossing the ice in the morning. There was no point in waiting any longer. They would make it across and home or die in the attempt. With Iliana snuggled up in his arms, he vowed to do everything in his power to get her back to Domiq. *Someday our children will grow up in that place*, he promised himself.

Chapter Twelve

As Kat and Lana enjoyed their breakfast, the sound of stomping feet outside the front door startled them. They were both surprised to see J.T. had arrived. He wasn't expected to come until lunchtime so Lana hurried to fix him something to eat.

"Don't worry about me," he laughed, "I had breakfast hours ago back at the station. There was nothing going on back at the village so I thought I'd come early to avoid anything that might arise needing my attention. Now they'll just have to wait until we get back."

Helping himself to a biscuit and some coffee, he brought them up to date on the local news involving a lost puppy and an angry moose mama. Seems someone had gotten a bit too close to her baby and she'd gone on a rampage kicking over log piles. He managed to make the story sound funny to them and soon they were all laughing.

"Sounds like I missed a good joke," Alexei said from the doorway. "Care to fill me in?"

Hearing the sound of his brother's voice, J.T. choked on his coffee and turned red in the face.

"What...when did you...," J.T. gasped as he stared at Alexei.

"I came in a couple of nights ago, and I see you're still trying to woo your women using our mother's cooking," Alexei smirked at his brother.

"That's enough," came Lana's sharp response. "We have a guest."

Turning to Kat, she patted her hand as she made an effort to apologize for her sons' lack of manners, "or should I say 'son'" she said pointedly looking at Alexei.

Kat decided silence was the best answer to her embarrassment at being categorized by Alexei as one of "J.T.'s women". There was obviously something going on here that went beyond sibling rivalry. The air was thick with hostility between the two of them. She was also confused to J.T.'s change in status from old friend of the family to 'son'. He certainly hadn't acted like a man with his mother on their first visit to Domiq.

"If you two intend to argue," Lana fumed, "You need to take it outside. I don't want to hear anymore."

She got up and began to clear the table. Taking the hint, Kat started to help her as the room filled with silence beyond the clattering of dishes. Without another word, Alexei headed out the back door as J.T. sat there staring at the table. He knew any disagreement between the two of them would leave him on the losing end. His status in this family was based on charity and blood always seemed to win.

Finally, he stood up and headed outside. If he couldn't handle his brother as family, he could certainly confront him in his role as peace officer on the isle. The rumors were flying in the village and J.T. was tired of trying to cover for his brother. He wanted to make sure everything going on at Domiq was on the up and up. He carefully avoided looking at Kat as he left. *Leave it to Alexei to ruin his chances with another woman*, he thought bitterly.

As the back door slammed behind him, Lana stood there looking sadly after her sons. She sighed and turned to Kat, thinking some kind of explanation was needed. The young woman looked just as sad as she tried to make sense of all this. She didn't want to end her visit on such a negative note.

"Don't worry, my dear. You're not the first woman to find yourself crosswise between those two. Let's go in the sitting room and I'll try to explain," Lana said taking her arm.

Kat studied the pictures on the walls as they walked looking for J.T.'s face. She didn't see a single photograph to confirm his status.

"You're looking for J.T.," Lana said watching her.

"Yes, I was wondering why I don't see any photos of him on these walls if he's your son," Kat confessed. "There are plenty of pictures of Alexei."

"J.T.'s not really my son. His mother was from the village and she fell for an American soldier on a trip to Anchorage. Just after J.T. was born, his father was killed in an accident and she came back here to live with family. She wasn't taking care of J.T. and one day I went down to the village and saw him picking through the trash. I brought him home with me. He was five or six by then and thin as a rail."

"That must have been awful," Kat said.

"It was hard, but in some ways it was worse for Alexei. He wasn't ready to share his home with another child and the two of them clashed almost daily for a long while. When they started going to school in the village, they competed in everything, sports, grades, girls, you name it, and they fought over it. I was struggling with my own grief after the death of my husband, Alexei's father, and I just wanted peace.

"Finally, I broke down and sent Alexei away to a boarding school. I kept J.T. here with me as I had no legal rights over him. That actually worked to resolve the conflicts between them and they eventually developed a kind of truce. I was lulled into thinking they'd become brothers."

"Unfortunately, their truce ended their nineteenth summer when Alexei came home for the school break. J.T. was dating a girl from the village and brought her out here almost every day. They were talking marriage and I was looking forward to grandchildren. The girl took one look at Alexei and fell head over heels for him. She was like a little puppy following him around the house. It all ended badly and the fight they had nearly cost Alexei his life, as he fell over a cliff in the midst of it. J.T.'s guilt kept him away for a long time and Alexei ran away soon after with a scar to remind him of his brother.

"The past couple of years, I was working on reconciliation with both of them and felt I was making progress. J.T. started coming out here with Marissa, who he was dating at that time. When Alexei came to visit, history repeated itself and the only thing that prevented them from killing each other this time was the clear understanding that Marissa was simply a gold-digger looking for the best deal. I managed to convince J.T. that Alexei had done him a favor."

"Ah, that explains a few things," Kat said leaning back in her chair. "I've heard Marissa arguing with J.T. at school. I never heard what they were arguing about."

"Yes, Alexei wouldn't give her the time of day and she's done everything she can to get her claws into him," Lana mused. "At least J.T. wised up to her pretty quickly and broke it off. She's not his type anyway."

"I'm confused about one thing," Kat hesitated, "does J.T. think that we're dating or something?"

"No, I don't think so," Lana replied, "unless he's seeing you beyond bringing you here. I thought he was bringing you out here for my sake. He's worried that I'm out here all alone too much of the time. I'm not sure he's ready to risk his heart on love again."

Kat gave a sigh of relief as there was nothing in J.T.'s actions to suggest otherwise. She would chalk up Alexei's remarks as a jab at this brother and nothing more. She certainly didn't see herself in the role of a gold-digger. She'd come to this isle hoping to escape the matchmaking efforts of other people. It would be ironic to step into the role of trying to force a relationship here of all places.

"Kat, we need to head back to the village," J.T. spoke from the doorway startling them both. "I have some things I need to do and I'm sure you need to get ready for school tomorrow."

Kat nodded and stood up to gather her things. She was relieved to see that J.T. didn't appear to be overly upset. A repeat of the ride out here wasn't something she'd been looking forward to. The ragged old UTV probably wasn't up to many such rides and they'd find themselves walking.

Lana walked with them to the door, holding onto J.T.'s arm. He reassured her several times that everything was okay before they left. She pressed Kat to come back the next weekend so they could finish reading the journal. J.T. looked interested at her words, but didn't ask about the matter. *It probably didn't have anything to do with me anyway*, he thought to himself.

As they headed back to the village, Kat turned and waved good-bye to Lana. A quick scan of the house didn't reveal anyone watching from the window. She wondered where Alexei managed to disappear to at such times. She'd thought she'd seen the whole lodge by this time and there weren't that many rooms for a person to hide. *Perhaps he had a secret cave*, she thought to herself. *That would explain the rumors of a pirate she'd heard.*

***

Ulriq used the sun, the moon and the stars to set their course across the ice. There were no other ways he could keep them headed in the right direction. He had no distant mountains or other land masses and the ice was never the same from one year to the next. With little experience to go on, he kept checking his direction by looking backwards until the land behind was no longer visible.

On the third day, an ice fog started building up around them and it became harder to see where they were going. This forced them to slow their pace as he searched carefully for cracks and crevices that might cause them to fall or break through the ice. The creaking and popping sounds kept their nerves on edge and Iliana needed more time to rest each time they stopped. He feared she was falling ill as their food was running out.

The fifth night was the worst as an icy wind blew straight at them, pulling and tugging at their clothes. Finding a hollowed out place big enough for them to crawl inside, Ulriq placed some furs inside and then with Iliana snuggled down, he wrapped himself around her trying to keep her warm. He feared the cold was going to defeat them on this night and closed his eyes in frustration, hoping death would come quickly.

In the darkest part of the night, Ulriq tried to turn himself a bit as he felt too warm. Confused at the warmth pressing against his back, he started to squirm, but a voice at his ear shushed him. Feeling safe, he fell back asleep and the two of them awoke with a renewed sense of hope. Marveling at the warmth of their small cave, Iliana praised Ulriq's choice of sleeping quarters.

"I can't take credit for this," Ulriq confessed. "Look!"

Iliana turned to see what he was pointing at and saw a few long, white hairs frozen into the ice around the cave.

"What is it," she asked wrinkling her nose.

"I think Nanuq, the great white bear came and lay down next to me last night. He kept us warm and saved our lives."

Iliana's eyebrows rose up and she stared at Ulriq in surprise. He stood up and looked around the area. There was no sign of the bear in any direction. He couldn't even find any footprints in the snow. Shrugging his shoulders, he thought maybe it had all just been a dream. Who would believe such a story anyway?

Repacking their sled, they tried to ignore the growling of their stomachs. The last of their food was eaten for lunch yesterday. Ulriq had no idea of what they could find to eat out here on the ice. They started walking without talking. They hadn't gone very far when Iliana spotted a fish frozen into the ice. Pointing it out to Ulriq, the two of them laughed as he poked and pried it free from its prison.

"Breakfast is served, my princess," Ulriq said as he sliced some fillets off the fish.

The two of them walked on happily munching on the unexpected bounty. This day was getting off to a very good start. Their hearts were light as wind.

By the end of that day, the first island was within sight. Ulriq was no longer concerned with finding the direction and focused his attention on the ice. The cracks and crevices were still a threat, but the ice appeared solid for as far as they could see. They found another hollowed out ice cave and settled in for the night.

As the night before, Ulriq awoke in the middle of the night to find himself pressed into the warm cave by a large furry body. He made no effort to escape this time, but easily fell back to sleep. He was thankful for the kindness of Nanuq and the legacy of his father. Their lives were spared by the two of them.

They reached the first island on the sixth day. The people living there were surprised at their appearance. Many of them were the villagers from the isle and they recognized Ulriq after a time. They were very surprised to hear his story of traveling across the ice. Many of them gathered to hear their tale and plied them with food as they talked.

The next morning, they headed across the ice to home. It wasn't very far in light of the distance they'd gone before and they made land well before dark. Ulriq went first to inquire of his mother and found her well. Her husband didn't speak to them, but stared at the two of them suspiciously. He didn't want to believe her son had returned. It was almost as if Ulriq had died in his mind.

They decided to stay in the village that night and head out to Domiq in the morning. No one in the village seemed to know anything about the condition of the lodge. Ulriq's mother just looked at him and shook her head when he asked her. The lodge was irrelevant to them.

At least the villagers had food this year. His mother fed them both, pushing extra food at Iliana as she eyed her daughter-in-law's belly without saying anything more. Neither of them caught on to her interest.

Chapter Thirteen

Kat found herself thinking about Ulriq and Iliana several times during the next week. She marveled at the kind of love that could bridge the gap between a Russian princess and a simple man. Sharing bits and pieces of the story with her students, she could see their interest growing.

Their world was quite small and no one thought much about walking across the ice. They'd been told their whole lives it was dangerous or even impossible. Besides, they had planes and helicopters and snow machines. What kind of crazy person would go walking out there on the ice with polar bears and all the other dangers?

She told them about the lodge and how it had been built by a Russian trader with trees from the mainland. Most of them had only seen it from afar. It was like a whole other world from the small village they lived in and yet it was only a short ride away on J.T.'s UTV.

Kat wondered at the events that kept the people in the village away from the lodge. Perhaps the answer lies in the journal. She hoped that nothing would keep her from finishing reading the rest of the story.

By Friday afternoon, she was happy to head back to the lodge with J.T. She was relieved to see his face appear in the doorway as the last student was heading out.

"Are you ready," he asked. "I've got to get you out there and hurry back. I've got a 'situation'" he said with a shy grin.

"From the look on your face," Kat teased, "I'd say it's more like you've got a 'date'!"

J.T. just grinned a bit wider as he handed her a helmet. She was happy for him.

Lana was waiting at the door for them when they drove up. She looked as excited about their arrival as Kat and waved them anxiously inside. Giving both of them a welcoming hug, she looked surprised when J.T. explained that he had to go right back.

"I hope everything's all right," Lana said as she walked inside with Kat.

"Everything's fine," Kat said, "he's got a date!"

The two of them looked at each other and smiled.

"Do you know who he's dating," Lana asked.

"No, but I'm sure it's not Marissa," Kat said. "I saw her heading off with Jim after work. I think they're back together or something."

"That's a relief," Lana sighed.

The two of them headed right to the sitting room. Lana had a steaming pot of cocoa and a plate of freshly made cookies already set up.

"I was hoping you would read a bit and then we'll have some supper," she said. "Is that okay with you? I'm dying to know what happens to them."

"Me too. I couldn't stop thinking about them all week. I even shared some of the story with my students." Kat hesitated. "I hope that's okay with you."

"Of course! This is really a story that belongs to the whole isle. After all, Ulriq was the son of a great leader and may have become a leader in his own right. We have to finish the story to find out."

Picking up the journal, the two of them sat down and got ready to read.

"Whoa! Wait a minute! You're not starting without me, are you," came a voice from the doorway.

Kat looked up to see Alexei coming into the room. She was surprised to find him still here even though this was his home. She thought he'd gone off somewhere 'pirating".

His mother gave him a pleased smile and motioned for him to sit next to her. With everyone settled, Kat found her place and started to read.

***

As they drew near to the lodge, Ulriq searched for signs that anyone had been in the area. There weren't any tracks and the snow lay unbroken before and around the building. The silence was broken only by the howling of the wind coming in over the ice as they struggled through the deep snow with their small sled.

Ulriq's mother had given them some food, but he knew it would be up to him to find more for them. Since Iliana's father was intending to buy the supplies they needed for the winter, there was very little here in the house for them. He knew they were still facing some challenges if they were to make it through the winter. The one thing he didn't know was that soon there would be another mouth to feed.

Their son was born during the earliest part of spring just after the birds arrived. The proud parents told him many stories as he was growing up, but his favorite one was how they'd traveled across the ice. He learned all of their stories by heart so he could tell them to his own children some day for that was the way of the People.

Chapter Fourteen

Kat paused and looked up at the others.

"There's not much more here," she said. "I can make out some names and dates that seem to be a list of the family photos Iliana brought from Russia."

"It's an amazing story," Lana said quietly. "I think we all know how it ended. Their son, my grandfather married my grandmother and they had two children..."

"Two children," Alexei asked.

"Yes, my mother and my uncle. He was a soldier and died in the war. My mother married my father and *they* had two children..."

"You have a brother or a sister," Kat asked.

"I had a brother. He died in an accident when we were children. It was never explained to me," Lana said sadly. "My mother said there was a curse on this family over the men, but I don't believe it."

"Neither do I," Alexei added with a gentle smile. "Otherwise, I wouldn't be here, now would I?"

"Well, you nearly weren't here," Lana retorted. "If it hadn't been for J.T., you would have died that day. Thank God, he learned how to swim!"

"What happened, if I may ask," Kat said.

"When Alexei and J.T. were fighting over that girl, this one fell over the cliff and into the sea. J.T. dove into the sea after him and pulled him out. He'd gashed his face open pretty badly and the two of them came home covered in blood. I nearly passed out at the sight of them," Lana grimaced. "It was a pretty scary time for all of us."

"Well, it definitely adds to his mystique as a pirate," Kat laughed.

The two of them stared at her in shocked silence.

"Uh...I mean..," Kat mumbled.

Alexei broke out laughing.

"You think I'm a pirate," he barely got out before laughing some more.

"Sorry," Kat said. "It's just something my students told me. I didn't really believe them, but I saw the lights out in the Strait and then you appeared at the house..."

"Is that what the people in the village think about my son?"

"I, uh, can't speak for everyone, but really, it's just a bunch of silly rumors," Kat broke off her words and looked at them helplessly.

"I like the idea of being a pirate, but I'm sorry to tell you the truth is so much less exciting. I'm an oceanographer. I have a small, private submarine and my job is to map the underwater currents in this region. That's why we have small groups of guests in and out of here. They're scientists and researchers using the data I gather to further their studies."

"Oh!" Kat sat back in her chair feeling very silly. She couldn't have been more wrong about something if she'd tried. It had never occurred to her to simply ask him about his work like people would do normally. She'd just gone with the assumption the rumors were true.

Lana stood up and said it was time to make them all something to eat. She headed to the kitchen.

"Kat, would you be willing to translate Iliana's journal into English for us? I'd be willing to pay you whatever you think is fair. My mother would so much appreciate it," Alexei added, hoping to convince her to say yes.

Kat thought that was a wonderful idea. She would have done it without any payment at all, but she didn't want to insult him for offering.

"I'll do it on one condition," she ventured.

"What's that?"

"That you come to the school and do a presentation for my class about your work as an oceanographer."

Alexei thought about it for a moment and then stuck out his hand.

"Deal!"

"Great! I'll set up a date and do some pre-teaching so they can ask good questions. I think they'll love meeting a real pirate, uh, oceanographer," she grinned. "By the way, where do you keep your ship, sub?"

"I thought you read it in the journal. There's a series of caves here and one of them is under the house. It opens out to the sea during the lowest tides and it's like having a private parking garage. It's a perfect place for a submarine. We try to keep it pretty secret, because of military concerns mainly. J.T. tends to worry about it more than anyone since he's charged with keeping the peace out here."

"So how will you be able to share that with my students?"

"I'm not going to ruin all of their mysteries. I'm only going to tell them about the ocean currents and how that affects them. The submarine is a tool. The location, well, that's on a need to know basis, if you get my drift."

Kat looked at him blankly as he grinned back at her.

"Sorry. Bad oceanographer joke...drift...get it?"

Kat swiped a hand over her head and groaned.

"Right over my head. Hope my students are a bit quicker."

A call from the kitchen let them know supper was ready.

***

Each winter, Ulriq would take his son on the Great Hunt with the villagers. Nanuq no longer came to give a tally, but it didn't matter. There were so few families left in the village, their hunt was far smaller than ever before. They'd gone back to the old way of taking only what they needed to survive.

Some of the villagers pressed him to come back and be their leader, but Ulriq wanted no part of it. His heart for the People had changed and he no longer felt like he could lead them. Most of the Elders had died or left and the village was full of strange faces to him.

When his mother died, his last connection to them was severed and he stayed away from the village more and more. His life was at Domiq with Iliana and his son. His skill at carving ivory brought him a small measure of fame with the oriental traders. This gave them some freedom to trade for food and other goods. Their simple life provided them with all that they needed to be happy.

Their son was twelve when Nanuq came to talk to him while he walked alone on the rocks one day. He hurried home to tell his father the words of the great white bear. Ulriq warned him never to speak of this to anyone else. The old ways had been forgotten and no one wanted to be reminded of what had been lost. This story was for their ears alone to hear.

Epilogue

Kat pressed through the crowd trying to get to her gate in the busy airport.

"Kat! Kat!"

A voice calling her name in the crowd caused her to stop and look around. Suddenly, she caught sight of a familiar face.

"J.T.! Look at you," she crowed spotting him with a baby on one arm and a little girl hanging off his trouser leg. She hurried over to get a closer look.

"I see you've been busy."

J.T. blushed and grinned at her. He made the introductions as his wife came up and rescued the baby hanging off his arm.

"What are you doing here in Anchorage," he asked.

"I'm just passing through. I'm on my way home from Russia again. I have to leave every few months because of the visa deal."

"Ah, yes. I get it," J.T. said.

"So, how's your mother doing? I bet she loves being a grandmother. She told me once how important it was to her."

"She's good and you're right. She's a wonderful grandmother. She comes down to the village once a week to volunteer at the school and our children spend a lot of time at the lodge with her. I know she'd love to see you and hear about your adventures in

Russia. We all would."

"That's not a bad idea. I'll have to take a look at my schedule and figure out how to work that in, but I'm sure it can be arranged," Kat said. "How does Alexei like being an uncle?"

"I think he likes it," J.T. admitted. "By the way, he's working with this movie producer to have Iliana's journal made into a movie. He said that if this happens, you'll get full credit for your work. You could be famous some day!"

Kat laughed at the look on his face.

"I don't think translators get to be famous. It's just nice to get a mention in a real movie. I'm sure it will be wonderful. The story certainly changed my life. It gave me the incentive to learn more about my origins and my own history. It's slow going over there, but the people do love to tell their stories. I've really enjoyed my work in recording them for future generations."

An announcement over the loudspeaker broke into their conversation.

"Oh no, that's my flight," Kat said. "I've got to go. It's been great meeting your family. I'll see what I can do with my schedule and get in touch with Lana about visiting."

Giving her a quick hug as a send-off, J.T. stood and watched her go once again. He knew she probably wouldn't come for a visit. Lana had asked her several times. It was clear to all of them, the young woman was in search of something that went far beyond Yesterday.

THE END

I hope you enjoyed this story.
If you would leave a review on Amazon
it would be greatly appreciated!

Sincerely,
Renee Hart

About The Author

Renee Hart was born in Fairbanks, Alaska.
She has lived in the Alaska Bush for the past
12 years and enjoys nature, quilting, baking,
and writing stories that draw from her
life experiences.

CPSIA information can be obtained
at www.ICGtesting.com
Printed in the USA
LVOW11s0325140218
566428LV00001BB/161/P